Happy Christmas

by

Robin Langford

Book Cover and Illustrations by Robin Langford

I

*This is dedicated to all
who love Christmas.*

Happy Christmas

Snowflakes

The dark blue night sky gradually became white, and a blanket of stars fell all over the streets and houses as snowflakes. Brilliant yellow lights were visible through the thick white snow; young faces peeped through curtains, filled with wonder and expectation, while figures hurried to their warm homes and late suppers. All the sounds became more and more muffled, and the harsh realities became soft and enchanting.

In a town square, a bright warm light shone from a small café. Two couples inside, by their flickering candles, didn't notice the snow build up on the window-panes as they talked quietly and intimately, oblivious to everything around them, while the elderly café owner watched kindly over them making sure that all was well. He then noticed the falling snowflakes outside and smiled as his eyes lit up with excitement; when he was little, his parents had told him that the snow fell to keep the world warm at Christmas, so ever since then he had always loved the snow.

Slowly, he made his way over to the bay window and looked out; it took him back to his youth, back to the days when all dreams were possible. On such a night he had met his wife, Katya, all those years ago. It also had been Christmas Eve - they had met in a café - this one in fact, both shy and awkward young things, both looking for someone.

He watched the snow falling lighter and lighter until it stopped; the street was quiet now, nothing moved. As he was about to turn away, he noticed a slim huddled figure moving smoothly across the snow towards his small café; he shuffled over to the door to welcome them in out of the cold.

As the person crossed the threshold, he closed the door behind them and then helped them off with their hat and coat. Out from under the hat cascaded a head of golden and russet hair, and as he looked at the face, his heart missed a beat; she was beautiful, so like his wife Katya those many, many years ago. The girl looked at him and gave him a slight smile; he took her things, hung them up and then led her over to the window table, near the warm fire. As she sat down, the light from the candle bathed her face in a soft glow.

His mouth opened automatically, asking her what she would like to eat and drink. She hesitated for a moment and then asked for a pot of tea, and some hot honey cakes. He walked away and gave the order to the headwaiter; it was funny, he had known the order she was going to give practically before she had said it.

She sat at the table, sipping her warm drink and eating the hot cakes, while every now and then looking out of the bay window into the street with a feeling of suppressed excitement. Was she expecting someone? Was she meeting them here? The elderly host found himself being drawn to the front door and looking out too. For what, he did not know, but he also was feeling an excitement deep within.

Now and then he glanced back to the young girl; she was so, so beautiful. Not since Katya had gone had he felt such an intense wonder; all the old memories came flooding back, their love, their heartaches, their dreams all rolled together. Forever they had promised to love and together they had sworn to die. Many, many times he had wished he had died with her, but it was not meant to be. Life had left him empty, with a feeling of numbness when she had passed; it had no real meaning without her - his heart began to ache with the longing for relief, he wanted his happiness back, he wanted his Katya back. Her voice whispered inside his head, *"Rudi, I will always love you,"* and he imagined that slight smile which had captivated him so completely; his eyes filled with tears. With a shaky hand he took out his handkerchief, wiped them away, blew his nose and stood at the front door, waiting.

Suddenly, a lone figure ran up to the door and pushed it open, taking him by surprise. A young man stepped inside and stamped on the doormat as if his feet were cold.

The old man helped him off with his hat and coat and then asked him where he would like to sit. The young man looked around and then boldly went over to the young girl's table,

"May I sit at your table? It is delightfully warm here and I should very much like the company. Would you mind...?"

The girl looked at him for a moment and then nodded. Rudi looked on - he had been impetuous like that once. The two of them seemed awkward at first, but they soon became friendly as she looked out of the window less and less, and more and more at the young man. Their conversation was so soft and muted that Rudi could only see them mouthing their words. He went over and asked the young man,

"May I get you something to eat or drink?"

"Yes, please. A hot chocolate and a few hot cakes, thank you so much," he said, his eyes now sparkling with happiness.

After a few more drinks and cakes they both started to laugh and relax, but to Rudi, it seemed as if he were watching a silent film.

The evening was getting late and the two other couples had left already; the waiters began to leave too, it was near midnight and they wanted to get back to their homes and families. The young couple were so rapt in each other now, that it was only when the headwaiter told them that the café was closing that they realised that they had to leave. Rudi went over to the front door, handed the young man his coat and hat and then reached for the young girl's. As he helped her on with it, he felt a warm glow flow through him - he handed her the hat. The young couple looked at him and then at each other; they had so much love in their eyes. The clock chimed twelve. He opened the door for them and they left silently together, walking away arm in arm, out and over the newly fallen snow. As he watched them, he noticed that they made no footprints; he smiled, he felt so happy.

"Monsieur Rudi, Monsieur Rudi," the headwaiter cried out loud as the old man collapsed gently to the floor, *"Mon dieu!! He is dead!"*

Happy Christmas

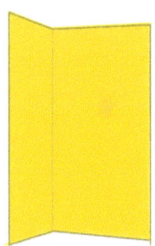

The Tear

She looked at the inside of the Christmas card; it was blank. She then flipped back to the front; there was a happy family scene, captured in time, with all their presents laid out in front of a nice warm fire. A Christmas tree was hung with glitter and sweets of all kinds, and the children looked lovingly up at their parents, who were reaching out to hug them; this was something she had always dreamed of, a family of her own.

Her childhood days had lacked any real kindnesses; an orphan, with no parents reaching for her to give a hug and a kiss. Sometime ago, there had been someone who had cared about her, for a brief time. His ways had always been kind and gentle; in fact he had been too kind and too gentle for her. Alone she felt she could cope; no need to give or take, no responsibilities. Her eyes glanced back to the picture on the front of the card - *oh, how she wanted that!* To be loved; to give love, to be happy. Why was there no writing inside? How strange!

As she opened the card again and moved it towards a side-light she saw a small smudge; she lifted it nearer to the light and examined it more closely. It was as if a tear had fallen on it and dried. Her sadness disappeared - *it was a tear!* She rushed to the telephone, dialed a number and waited.

"Hallo," said a man's gentle voice.

"It's me," she said.

"Did you get my card?" he said apologetically, *"I'm sorry I didn't write anything in it, there was…nothing I could think of to say."*

"You did say something," she said with a break in her voice.

"Will you...?" he paused.

"Yes," she cried, *"I'll be right over."*

Happy Christmas

Happy Christmas

The Snowflake

Happy Christmas

One minute
Before Christmas,
And high on a hill,
A star stood large
And perfectly still,
As moonbeams shone
From a dark satin sky
Spreading their beams
Onto shadows so high.
Everything was waiting
For the silent snow fall,
And nothing seemed to want
To move at all,
'Twas as if the night
Were holding its breath…
(Even the Owl
Delivered no death
As a mouse scuttled
Disturbing the peace
And then realised
T'would do better
To cease).

The air was crisp
And had a slight chill,
But behind it all
There was a huge thrill
For there was
Magic this night
And a wish to fulfill -
As was told in the book
The Legends of Old…

…All over the world
People looked
To the heavens,
Hoping that night
Good luck would be theirs,
And that they would be rich
And so would their heirs.

Like the bold Mr. Gold
So gross and so fat
(His head was so big
There wasn't a size
He could wear for a hat)
Who bought a building
Where there nested a stork
(Which he soon moved on)
In the heart of New York -

He bought all the buildings
That rivaled its height
And banned all the planes
From flying that night -
(He banned them at least
From flying that way)
Just in case they blew
The Snowflake astray.

Or the Smedley-Smooth
In her London mews,
Who thought it a ruse
For her to use
Her maid called "Kitty,
Kitty Goodshoes,
To stand on the balcony

Instead of her
Out in the cold for it
(Tho' wrapped in fake fur).
Not knowing that the maid
On catching the flake
Would wish lots of wishes
And off she would make,
Off over there
To a foreign clime
And never, never work
'Til the end of time.

Mr. Thin & Ms. Plain
(Known by some
As the Pin & Pain)
Had shown their cunning
With a huge great kite
Which they already
Had put in flight.
For it flew up high
From a church's steeple
Way above
The ordinary people,
So if the flake
Were to fall that way
It would catch it carefully
And they'd wish away -
(He'd be fat
And she'd be cute,
Tho' whether or not
It both would suit).
Together they sat
Gazing on high
Up to the stars
With a hopeful sigh.

There was
Mr. and Mrs.
Ha Pi Fat,
Whose son
Was called
La Zi Fat,
(For all
He seemed
To do all day
Was to sit and eat,

Not work or play).
They saw that when
They were old and grey
He'd still do nothing
Every day.
For many years
They had despaired
And in many ways
Their views had aired,
So when they heard
Of this wondrous tale -
In hope they sat
On a mountain top
That into their bowl
The flake would plop.

Even Ministers and Presidents
Around the world
Conspired, intrigued
And set their plans
To have the Snowflake
In their hands -
Using secret planes
And 'copters too,
Rockets and beams
To seize their dreams.

While,
Bishops and Priests
Nuns and Vicars
Knelt to pray
In their Sunday knickers,
Hoping that prayer
Would divert its motion
Towards their saintly
Churches and towers,
And give them spiritually
Unlimited powers.

News reporters
And 'telly' stations
Across the globe
Flashed revelations,
And had discussions
On this and that
And what would be
Its repercussions.

Astronomers with
Their big bug eyes
Looked through telescopes
And watched the skies
Searching for the magic flake
In the silent star filled lake,
Hoping to find
And upon it look
And then write it in
A hard-backed book.

Witch doctors
In darkened huts
Muttered spells
For village chiefs,
While chieftain wives
Looked to the sky
With huge great
Leaves standing by
Ready to catch it
If it fell
And make their chieftains
Happy and swell.

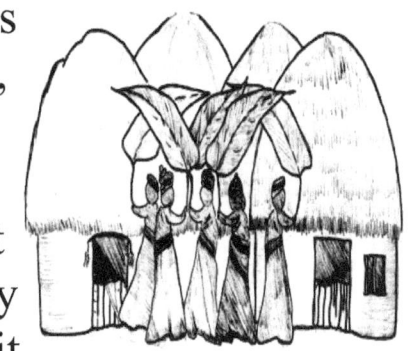

Artists also of various kinds
Meditated with their minds,
Whilst they sat
In dramatic positions
(Imagining making
Film decisions)
Compelling the flake
To fall their way
Through their Muse's
Hands that day.

Kings and Queens
In marble halls
Sent commands
From castle walls,
That should any
In their kingdoms
Catch the flake
They would - a Prince
Or Princess make.

Lovers with their
Hands entwined,
Stood on hills
(Having wined
and dined)
And gazed at the moon
And wondered if
The flake would fall
As a gift,
So that they could love
For all of time
And then life would be
One happy rhyme.

Meanwhile,
In a village small,
A family was huddled
In their hall,
Round a hearth
Which was well fired,
Their faces tearful
And looking tired -

Except for one
(Who in the shadows
Appeared the smallest)
Called, "Little One Fallows."
Now, Little One she
Had shed no tears
For being little
She held no fears,
She'd heard the others
Sniff and cry
And was curious to know
What and why,
There was no reason
She could find
(But then she since birth
Had been born blind).

She'd listened carefully
To what they'd said -
They seemed to say
That her father was dead,
No news had come
From the Northern Sea
Where he'd been diving
For a generous fee -

But she in her darkness
A year to this day,
Remembered him saying
He'd be there and away,
Back to his loves,
Back to his treasures,
Back to his home,
And ne'er again roam.
He'd whispered those words
Deep, into her dreams
And said he was travelling
On a 'magical' stream.
Nightly she'd wished
On that heavenly stream
That it would bring him home, safe,
On its wonderful beams,

With arms open wide
And so much to say
And happiness through
That one Christmas Day.
These nightly wishes
Kept the darkness at bay,
For when she was frightened
The darkness would play,
It would be blacker than pitch
Thicker than thick,
She would feel nearly dead
Very ill and quite sick -
And now with these fears
From all of the others
The darkness grew thicker
And determined to smother.
But then she remembered
His promise to come home,
And that he'd never again,
Never leave them alone -
She knew he'd come through
On that "magical stream"
As his voice had said softly
To her in her dream.

But far away
In a cold dark sea,
(Where every evil
In a dream could be)
Her father was trapped,
And his knee was shattered,
And the whole of his body
Was brutally battered.
Some rope was tangled
Round a rock
And webbing,
And his life was
Very quickly ebbing.
Air was bubbling
Leaking and lacking
As his hold on life
Was easily slackening.
Once let go
He'd remain below
Never to rise
From the murkiness there
Up to the love
Which wanted to care.
To die in agony
(As 'twas his fate)

No light, no love,
And all alone,
His family thrown
Out from their home -
He saw his loved ones
Cold and sad
And times for them
Gone worse to bad,
His wife weeping
'Til she died -
The children lost
And by her side.
In his mind
His anger grew,
And everything
'Gainst the rock
He threw,
His weight moved it
But not enough
For the rock was huge
And the rope was tough.
He looked up
Through the sea
To heaven,
Through the darkness
To the light

And asked that
If he died,
It might
Help his family
And see they should
Never want
For daily food.
Find happiness and love
In life's full pleasures
And love their father
Who'd loved his treasures,
Loved them 'til
His heart did burst,
And now it seemed
That he was cursed
Never to see
Those dear, dear faces
Which occupied
Such little spaces.
Salty tears began
To fill his mask,
So he pushed it up
And chok'd and gasped,
As the tears
Flowed into the deep
And his eyes slowly closed
To go to sleep.

The cottage clock
Chimed its note
And then the mother
Softly spoke
To her children, four.
"Well, my dears,
There's nothing more,
Off to bed,
Today is - Christmas
So say a prayer
To those who miss us,
Your father will
Be here I know
If it's meant to be,
So - we'll see."

The children left
With heavy feet
To their beds
To try and sleep.

Having put Little One
Up in the loft
On her bed
So sweet and soft,

The mother went down
On her bed to lie,
But all she could do
Was to weep and cry.

Now, Little One
Lay in her
Snug bed sack
And wondered when
Her father'd be back.
She didn't believe
That he was dead,
As all the rest
Of them had said.
She lifted herself
Out of bed
And opened the window
To breathe the air,
As she did nightly
Foul or fair.
She felt the moonshine
On her face
And imagined the stars
All over the place
Flashing as her father

Would always say
Like jewels in Paradise
For those who pray.
Then she put
Her hands together
And asked that
If God might,
Or, if God could
Send her father
Home to them, safe
And never leave,
(No never again)
Then the day
Would be
Christmas indeed
(And no presents or
Food would they need)
She wished the world then,
Could be as happy as they
On that wonderful
Christmas Day.
As she said this
And as she blew
Her prayer to heaven
And off it flew,

Into her hands
There softly fell
Something gentle -
And all seemed well.
She couldn't see
The white Snowflake
Fall like a star
From way up far,
She couldn't see
As her hands it touched
And around her body
A white light couched
Her tiny frame
In heavenly light
As though an angel
Of the night.
But through her darkness
She saw a stream -
A 'golden' stream
As she had dreamed,
And on its golden
Starry path
A figure stood
So happy and so good.

His arms were wide
With presents galore
For all the family
And many more
And then she heard him
Knock their door.
Little One always
Believing the best,
Jumped from the bed
With innocent zest
And ran down the stairs
With footing so sure,
And then lifted the latch
On the front door.
As it creaked
Slowly open wide,
She saw Father Christmas
Right outside, waiting
In a red-white suit
Silent as though
He were mute,
Looking unsure
As to what to do,
'Til with open arms
To him she flew,

And held him tight
With all her might
As though he were
A dream come true.
But then he
Suddenly disappeared,
And there instead -
Her 'father' appeared,
Looking at her
With such surprise,
For now he saw
She had blue eyes.
The prettiest blue eyes
He'd seen on another
(Except o'course
Those of her mother)
The rest of the family
With tears all dried away,
Came to see
What was at play
So early on
That Christmas Day,
And when they saw
Their father there,
And Little One

With 'happy eyes'
Showing herself
No surprise,
They knew that there
A miracle had been
Whilst they had slept
And had not seen.

"He came," she said
On the *golden stream* -
I know I saw it,
It wasn't a dream."

Now, remember she had wished
Happiness to all,
So over the world
Happiness *did* fall -

Mr. Gold
Became so happy
That he became
A 'generous' chappy ·

Smedley - Smooth
Kept her maid,
And on that day
Some tickets she paid
For 'em both to travel
To foreign climes,
As a couple of friends
Til the end of time -

Mr. Thin became
Rather round,
While Ms. Plain
Became rather vain
For she'd been turned
Into a pretty dame -

Mr. and Mrs. Ha Pi Fat
Concerned for their son
La Zi Fat
Changed his name
To, *Goo' Old Fat,*
And do you know
That was that -
For from that moment
'Til the day they died
He took such care of them,
With such deep pride.

So, all and everyone
On that day
Received some happiness
In their way
From the wish
Of that magical flake,
-

That fell from heaven
For a little girl's sake.

For more books by Robin Langford, go to:

A Story Company Publishing

www.astorycompanypublishing.com

www.ingramcontent.com/pod-product-compliance
Lightning Source LLC
Chambersburg PA
CBHW042320250626
47164CB00016B/61